T0143992

Happiness:

How To Recapture Yours!

Norma Faye Fox

AuthorHouse™
1663 Liberty Drive
Bloomington, IN 47403
www.authorhouse.com
Phone: 833-262-8899

This book is printed on acid-free paper.

ISBN: 978-1-6655-4478-8 (sc)
978-1-6655-4479-5 (e)

Library of Congress Control Number: 2021923498

Print information available on the last page.

Published by AuthorHouse 11/19/2021

authorHOUSE®

Instrumented by

Norma Faye Fox

"May God send His Devine Spirit to impart and assist in discerning this message to each individual need."

Dedication Page

To all the past, present and future "Angels Unaware "!

To my husband, Dale Fox...for all the joy and happiness he has given me!

To my father, Hargis Cletus Tolson...who passed away on June 18th, 2005...I miss conversations we had on the front porch every morning!

To my mother, Donna Pell Tolson Mays...for all her wisdom and loving support!

To my brother, William Mayo Tolson...for always reminding me to "Let It Happen Captain!"

To Robert Tolson Sr, who passed away on December 12th, 2020 from the covid virus, for always encouraging me to follow my dreams!

To my son-in-law, Rick Johnson and my grandson, Tony Ocasio... for all the Beautiful Illustrations for this book!

To my sister, Frances Tolson-Moss...for proofreading, editing and typing this manuscript...you'll forever be my Franchild!

To my daughter, Jessica Anne Johnson...who is always telling me to keep my chin up when the going gets too rough and for giving me eleven grandchildren: Tony, Timothy, Trevor, Trent, Abigail, Ricky, Shelby, Gavin, Sophia, LaBonita and Melodie...the pride of my happy heart!

To J. Hutchings...for giving me my sister "Pure Friend "!

A special thank you to my nephew, Adrian Tolson-Moss, for his contributions of illustrations!

And last, but not least...to Robert J. Titus, (Shaman WhiteFeather)... for teaching how to not let anyone or anybody ever steal your dreams!!!!!!!

Perhaps, once in a lifetime, a person has the opportunity to encounter someone who possesses the rare ability to encourage others. I count myself as fortunate to have known not one, but several of these "angels unaware." For others to recognize our hidden talents is indeed very gratifying. Yet bow often, if ever, does someone else come into our lives to point these features out to us? To reidentify our own attributes is often a difficult feat. To hold on to those qualities and groom them in the direction of acquiring one's dreams is even more demanding. Perhaps, this is best illustrated in the following story of Myriah. (Meer-ree-ah).

All of her life, Myriah wanted happiness, joy, acceptance, love. However, for the majority of her life, she existed in sadness and emptiness. The loneliness and hurt had formulated into an intense anger at the world.

She never wanted to stop caring about others, trying to understand what made them tick, or finding ways to relate to others at all levels in life. Yet that is exactly what she ended up doing. She stopped and became like so many other people who have stagnated.

She had grown up in a very strict environment. An environment that was molded by not only her parents, but it seemed to her, the entire world. Endless rules and regulations were a part of her everyday life. She was taught manners to the extent of forever being expected to take others into consideration with her every action or with her every word.

She followed the rules to the best of her ability, not so much out of thoughtfulness or kindness as it was to escape the wrath of her parents or the rejection of others. Someone along the line even had the forethought to suggest that in the absence of people in authority, if she ever let her guard down and disobeyed, that she would have to answer to God Almighty, Himself! This kept her minding her P's and Q's for a very long time.

Yes, scare tactics worked on her as a child. However, once she left the protection of the family fold, she gradually abandoned all those rules and regulations.

The only time Myriah felt really free was in the world of her imagination. No one else could penetrate the sacred isolated place that she had created within herself. Her mind existed in a universe of its own. She became a very private person, trusting her most inner thoughts to pencil and paper alone.

At various times in her life, she had attempted to share her aspirations with a selected few. She quickly learned to keep these thoughts to herself also. For she soon discovered that it was all too easy for others to shoot down her ideas before they even had a chance to develop into reality. Myriah absolutely abhorred being subjected to ridicule.

She could remember times when she did try to verbally express herself. More often than not, she would witness adverse reactions from others if she did not properly convey her thoughts.

It certainly didn't help matters any when she had to start using a retainer to keep her teeth straight. She develop a lisp so prominent that not even a speech therapist could help her get rid of it.

The emotional hang-up form this speech impediment hindered her tremendously in mastering the art of verbal communication. Lord help her, if she ever was upset over anything. She couldn't even get one word out then.

Nonetheless, it wasn't a total loss. She became a great listener. Even her observational skills were keenly sharpened. This seemed to enhance her perception of other people's feelings. For this she was grateful, because it gave her a special insight to her written words. Yet, it still wasn't enough for her.

She longed for a friend, someone she could share her thoughts with. Someone who knew her so well, that when she was upset, there wouldn't be any need for spoken words. Someone who loved her so much that they cared enough to find a way to reach her. She was tired of living in her own little world. She was also very lonely. She felt that she could be the best friend that anyone could ever hope for. The trouble was that there just didn't seem to be anybody that saw that potential in her. Or worse yet, they didn't care.

It was during those teenage years that she embarked upon an extensive search for this special friendship. Coupled with the intense desire to relate to others, along with the strong yearning of wanting to be accepted, to fit into this world somehow, some way that she traveled down the long road of disappointment, heartache, and despair. She wanted desperately to be understood and by the same token, to understand.

Understand. Than one word stood out above the rest because it was the one word that she heard the most, "You won't understand!"

A favorite story that was told about her was the one of when she was just a baby. Her first word was not Da-Da for Daddy. It wasn't Ma-Ma for Mommy. It wasn't even Ba-Ba for Bottle. She was often kidded that it was "Why?" As the old joke went, the other questions soon followed: What, Where, When, Who, and How?

Destined to become a journalist? She supposed so since that was her line of work. She definitely had a curious mind. Yet, she viewed herself as no different in that respect than any other child that ever existed. After she learned to read, she found a great many answers through the perusement of books. Still she couldn't relate to what it felt like to actually go through what she witnessed others go through. It was difficult to do so when she was as sheltered as much as she was. She grew tired of being told that she wouldn't "understand" because she personally never experienced any hardships.

Even though she was raised in a severe disciplinary manner, she could recall a childhood filled with wonderment, exciting discoveries and numerous adventures. She remembered looking forward to each new day because it would prove to bring new knowledge to learn.

Those fond memories did not come back to her until she took a child, who was at that time only two years old, on a nature walk. Every living plant, animal or insect opened up a whole new world to the child. The intriguing world of exploration. Myriah's adult world looked might drab compared to the excitement that was generated from the enlightening walk. She began to look back to her own childhood, wondering where she went wrong. When was it that she started down the path that led her to depression, a feeling of just a mere existence, with no apparent purpose whatsoever? What had transpired since her childhood? How did she ever lose sight of her dreams? Who was responsible For this occurrence?

Somewhere along the way, she had lost herself. Somewhere along the way, she had ceased being herself. When this happened, she grew into the miserable, lonely, depressed, hateful, irritable, and angry adult.

Bearing in mind that the only happiness or what she thought was happiness, was in her early childhood. She figured that was the place to start. What was it about her early childhood that sparked what she termed as happiness? When she was by herself, she could remember being at a liberty to imagine and pretend, to explore and discover her surroundings, and to create.

To the best of her ability, that was what mader her happy as a child. Now came the hard part. How could she recapture this happiness and apply it to the adult life? She tried to convert the words. To imagine and pretend would be to regain the use of her mind. To explore and discover would be to stop stagnating and learn new perspectives. To create would be to put her abilities and talents to use. Sounded simple. However, she was disappointed to find that it took more than imagination, pretending, exploration, discovery, and creation. So what was it that was stopping her from being happy?

Again, she looked back upon her childhood. She responded favorably to love, praise and rewards. She responded unfavorably to hate, ridicule and punishment. Yer why was it so important to her to win over the latter part? No matter how hard she tried to abide by the rules and regulations, it seemed never to be enough because there was always another rule or goal for her to strive for.

So back to square one. Less was expected from her as a child, this was true. The older she got, the more that was expected from her. How did she ever fall into that trap?

Obviously, it came from her need to feel accepted, appreciated, recognized, and loved. Subsequently, she fell into the trap of trying to please others.

Was this wrong? Yes, she surmised; because she had put her dreams, aspirations and goals on the back shelf and had forgotten all about herself. She had forgotten that she was an important person on this earth with her own contributions to give.

Why was this wrong? She concluded that whenever she did not meet up to everyone else's standards, she opened herself up to ridicule, rejection, and ultimately abandonment. She opened up herself to being used and tossed aside. Yet, she felt she only had herself to blame.

It wasn't until Myriah was 28 years old that she really grasped the root of her unhappiness. This great lesson came to her in the form of unconditional love. A young gentleman named Lemuel appeared in her life who was the epitome of how she wanted to become. Or as she surmised much later in life, to be what she already was but didn't know quiet how to make the real person within her emerge.

She admired him because he had managed to recapture the dreams of his youth and was on his way to actualizing them. Little by little, he revealed to her the secrets to his success.

"You've got to become one-minded," she recalled him saying with such clarity, "First, you start eliminating everything and anyone who isn't condusive to reaching your goals. I know it sounds kind of cold-hearted, but look at it this way. Let's say that five years down the line you have achieved your ambition. How are the people in your life now going to react to you? You're really going to be admired, aren't you?"

"Okay, now let's suppose that five years from now you haven't come any closer to your aspirations than you are to them at this moment. What is going to be the thought of you then? A hopeless dreamer? A loser? More importantly, how are you going to feel about yourself?"

"You mustn't let anything or anyone stand in your way of obtaining what you want out of life."

"The next step is to research. Find out just what it's going to take to achieve your objectives. Break it down into a step-by-step plan and then go for it with all you've got!"

Their relationship flourished and after a year it leveled out. In a sense, they had reached a stagnating plateau. A painful re-evaluation was undertaken and the final decision was drawn. If they married, the possibility of children would crop up. How would they feel about themselves, each other, and towards the children if this alliance took place before they attained their individual goals? They could foresee themselves resenting the other for getting side-tracked and therefore their original perspective intentions being waylayed. It was agreed that each would go their separate ways in an added effort to consummate not only their dreams but each other in the span of two years. For them, it was an extra motivation to acquire their goals.

Such wisdom and fortitude it must have taken to endure those two years. Yet their lives have now been enriched and blessed with the knowledge that their dreams where finally realized. The foundation of their union was solidified by their foresight and perseverance. However, their story does not end there. They took what they had learned and passed it on to not only their children but also to others.

The lesson that Myriah learned from Lemuel can aide all of us in making our dreams a reality. We need to probe into the deep recesses of our minds to reclaim the lost hopes and dreams that we have allowed to be overshadowed. After establishing our goals, we must embark upon a set plan to achieve those dreams.

We must regain our ability to imagine, explore, discover, and create. Then we must reach out from our isolated world and teach others how to not let anyone or anything **ever** steal one's dreams.

By passing on the knowledge we acquire to others, it in turn becomes embedded within us and perpetuates our own happiness. Dreams really can come true. For Our Heavenly Father knows the desires of your heart, and His Love for you wants to see you Happy.

Printed in the United States
by Baker & Taylor Publisher Services